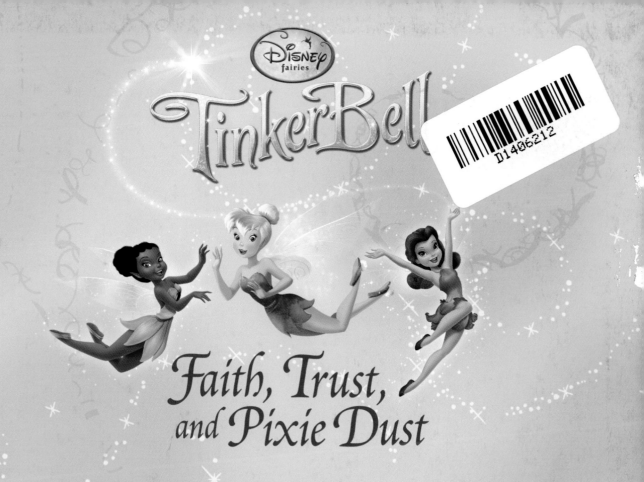

Disney fairies

TinkerBell

Faith, Trust, and Pixie Dust

Random House 🏠 New York

ISBN: 978-0-7364-2816-3

www.randomhouse.com/kids

MANUFACTURED IN SINGAPORE
10 9 8 7 6 5 4 3 2 1

Contents

Tinker Bell

A Guide to Pixie Hollow

By Elle D. Risco
Illustrated by Studio IBOIX and the Disney Storybook Artists

Close your eyes and imagine a magical land. . . .

A land where fairies use their special talents and a bit of pixie dust to put the finishing touches on nature. Flowers are painted by hand, snowflakes are individually frozen, rainbows are spun from water and sunshine—and all four seasons exist at once!

Here live the Never fairies of Never Land. Let them take you under their wings and show you around this wonderful place called Pixie Hollow!

Never Land

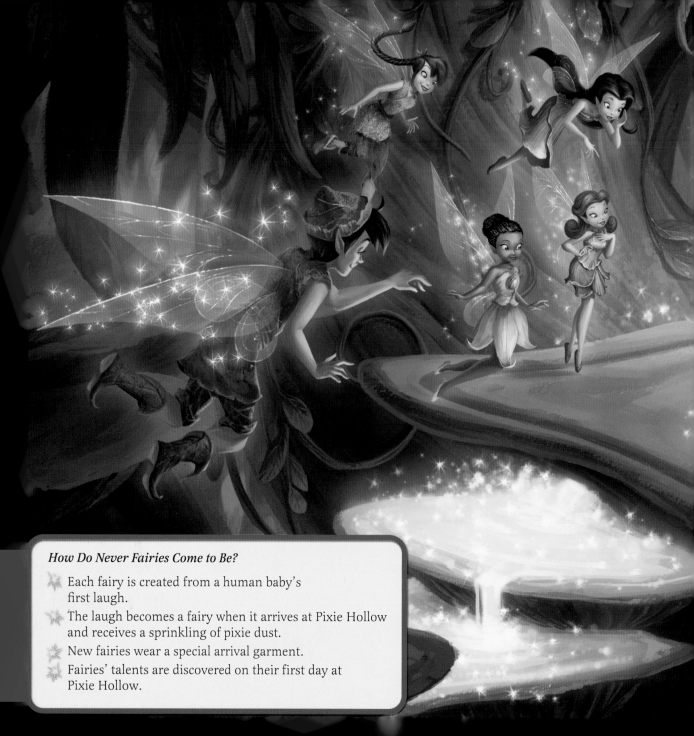

How Do Never Fairies Come to Be?

- Each fairy is created from a human baby's first laugh.
- The laugh becomes a fairy when it arrives at Pixie Hollow and receives a sprinkling of pixie dust.
- New fairies wear a special arrival garment.
- Fairies' talents are discovered on their first day at Pixie Hollow.

How does a fairy get to this tiny wonderland? It's easy! Just take flight and follow the Second Star to the Right. Ride the breeze, cross the sea . . . and before you know it, there you are!

Welcome to Tinker Bell's house! Like every fairy's home, Tink's is special in its own way. From her house, she has a great view of the tinker fairies' village.

Rosetta's House

Silvermist's House

Iridessa's House

Fawn's House

Meet Tinker Bell

❀ She's a tinker fairy who loves to invent things.

❀ She's determined, curious, and sometimes impatient.

❀ Look for her stylish leaf dress, green slippers, blond hair, and long bangs.

Lilypad Pond is the peaceful home of the water fairies. The sounds of lapping streams and tiny waterfalls are relaxing and musical. While touring the pond by leaf boat, you might see water fairies collecting dewdrops from spiderwebs or sculpting water like clay!

Meet Silvermist

- "Sil" is a water fairy who can talk to babbling brooks.
- She's encouraging, sympathetic, and quick to lend a hand.
- Look for her long, dark hair and her water-lily-petal dress.

The fields and meadows of Pixie Hollow are filled with colorful flowers and plants of every type that bloom here year-round. Gentle garden fairies can revive wilted blossoms with a sprinkling of pixie dust. These fairies also take care of young bulbs, making sure they get off to the right start!

Meet Rosetta

- Rosetta is as pretty as the roses in her garden.
- She's nurturing, and loves color, beauty, and sweet-smelling things.
- Look for her dainty rose-petal dress and shoes and her perfectly arranged red hair.

It's impossible to be anything but bright-eyed and lighthearted in Sunflower Meadow! Filled with sunflowers, this is the home of the light fairies. The sunbeams streaming through the golden petals are dazzlingly beautiful. Here, light fairies play jump rope with beams of light and gather sunlight in buckets!

Meet Iridessa

- "Dessa," a brilliant light fairy, is smart and organized.
- She creates and captures colorful rainbows!
- Look for her twinkling eyes, dark hair, and sunflower-petal skirt and shoes.

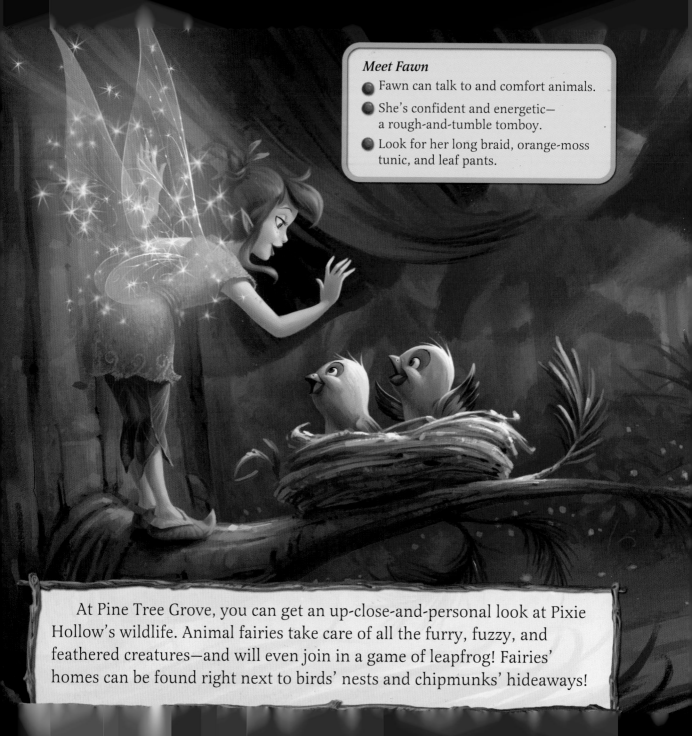

Meet Fawn

- Fawn can talk to and comfort animals.
- She's confident and energetic— a rough-and-tumble tomboy.
- Look for her long braid, orange-moss tunic, and leaf pants.

At Pine Tree Grove, you can get an up-close-and-personal look at Pixie Hollow's wildlife. Animal fairies take care of all the furry, fuzzy, and feathered creatures—and will even join in a game of leapfrog! Fairies' homes can be found right next to birds' nests and chipmunks' hideaways!

The best place to find fairies is the Pixie Dust Well, located in the Pixie Dust Tree at the heart of Pixie Hollow. At sunrise, every fairy comes here to get a daily dose of pixie dust. It's the perfect spot for fairies to catch up on gossip and talk about their plans for the day.

Meet Terence

✦ Terence is a dust-keeper fairy.

✦ He makes sure each fairy gets just the right dose of pixie dust—not too much, not too little.

✦ Look for his golden hair, acorn cap, and leaf vest.

One of Tinker Bell's favorite places is the tinkers' workshop in Tinkers' Nook. This is where tinker fairies carve acorn buckets, weave baskets, and fix wagons, pots, pans, and anything else that needs repairing. Tink is almost always here working on her newest inventions.

Berry/Nut Squasher

Berry-Paint Sprayer

23

Most of Pixie Hollow is safe and carefree. But there are a few things to watch out for.

First, avoid Needlepoint Meadow, where the Sprinting Thistles grow. These tall, prickly weeds race around, trampling or poking anyone in their path!

Second, beware of hawks! These fierce forest hunters can whisk away a fairy in an instant!

And third, watch out for Vidia. She's the only fairy who can ruin someone's day with one mean remark.

Meet Vidia

❀ Vidia is the fastest fairy in Pixie Hollow—
and she knows it.

❀ She lives by herself in a sour-plum tree.

❀ Impatient and conceited, Vidia is annoyed
by everyone.

While all four seasons exist at once in Pixie Hollow, it's the Never fairies who make the seasons change on the mainland. With each new season, the fairies have much to do.

As winter comes to an end and spring approaches, the fairies prepare everything from berry paint for coloring flowers to rainbow tubes full of rainbows. In a glorious procession, they carry their creations across the sea to bring the magic of spring to the world!

Other Highlights of the Year

- In winter, snowflake and frost fairies craft tiny details in ice crystals.
- In fall, the autumn fairies paint the bright yellow, orange, and red colors on all the leaves.
- In summer, the summer fairies chase dragonflies in green meadows bursting with sunshine!

There's so much to discover and explore in Pixie Hollow. You know the way—head toward the Second Star to the Right and fly straight on till morning. When you arrive, all your fairy friends will be waiting for you!

Disney fairies

TinkerBell
AND THE
LOST TREASURE

Tiny Adventurers

Adapted by Melissa Arps

Illustrated by Emilio Urbano, Manuela Razzi, Jeff Clark,
Dave Courtland, William Fenholt, and the Disney Storybook Artists

Do you like excitement and exploration? What about action-packed missions? If you said yes, then you're an adventurer just like Tinker Bell and her firefly friend Blaze! Tink's mission to find the enchanted Mirror of Incanta was one of her greatest adventures.

But there are some things to remember when setting out on a grand journey—take it from Tinker Bell!

Tinker Bell wrote down everything she planned to bring on her trip to the lost island north of Never Land.

- Map
- Compass
- Cheese
- Boysenberry rolls
- Pumpernickel muffin
- Pixie dust
- Pots and pans
- Sticks

Be Prepared

Make a checklist of all the items you'll need with you on your mission.

33

Tinker Bell built a cotton-ball balloon powered by pixie dust to take her on the long journey from Pixie Hollow.

Travel Smart

Whether you are traveling by land, sea, or air, be sure to have a safe mode of transportation.

Tinker Bell avoided a swarm of
fireflies being chased by a speedy bat.
She kept her balloon steady and on track.

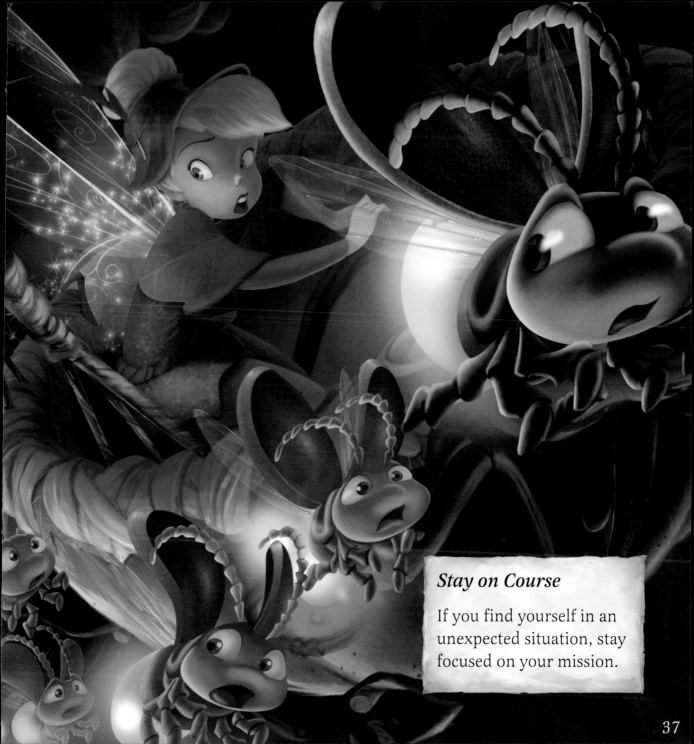

Stay on Course

If you find yourself in an unexpected situation, stay focused on your mission.

37

When Tinker Bell struggled to read her map in the dark, Blaze offered his light to help her see. She realized that the little firefly was a good friend to have on her journey.

Accept Help When You Need It

Even if you prefer to do things on your own, sometimes you might need a little assistance. Don't be afraid to accept help.

Tinker Bell is not the calmest fairy around—in fact, she is rather excitable. When she realized her balloon, compass, pixie dust, and supplies were all gone, she panicked and yelled at Blaze. But Tink settled down eventually. She had to continue on her mission.

40

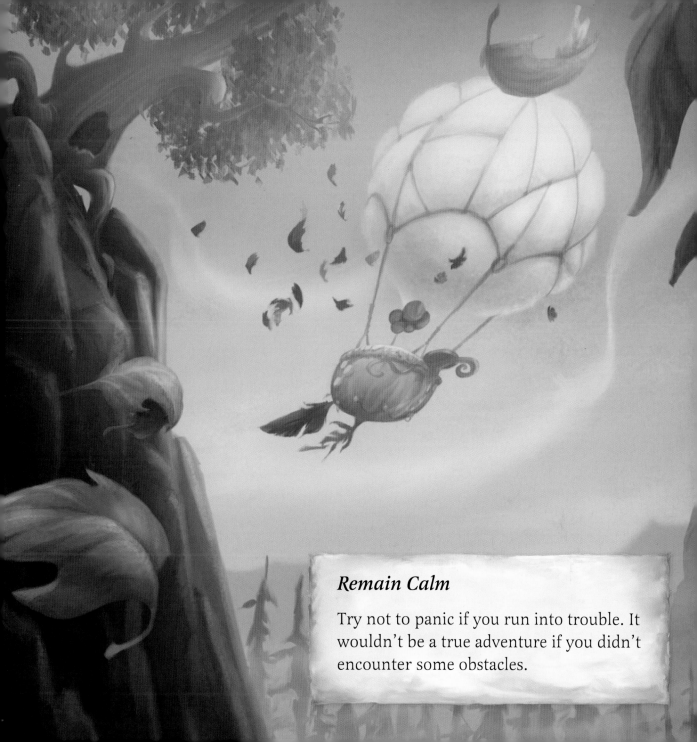

Remain Calm

Try not to panic if you run into trouble. It wouldn't be a true adventure if you didn't encounter some obstacles.

Blaze's friends gave Tinker Bell food and water when she needed it most. Fresh dew quenched her thirst, and honey filled her empty belly.

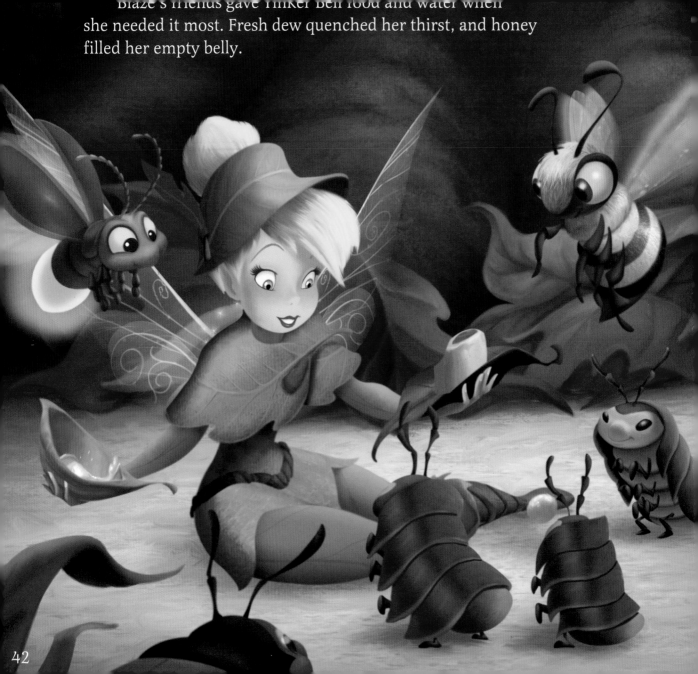

Keep Your Strength Up

Make sure you eat and drink on a long trip. Adventurers must stay strong and healthy.

Tinker Bell and Blaze sneaked past two arguing trolls and crossed the bridge that would lead them closer to their goal.

Go for It!

When you have a good chance to move forward on your mission— take it!

It was dark and spooky in the shipwreck. Winter Bell
removed her leaf headband and wrapped it around Blaze.
He became a flashlight and lit the way!

Be Creative

Got an idea? Make it happen! Work with the things you have to create something even better.

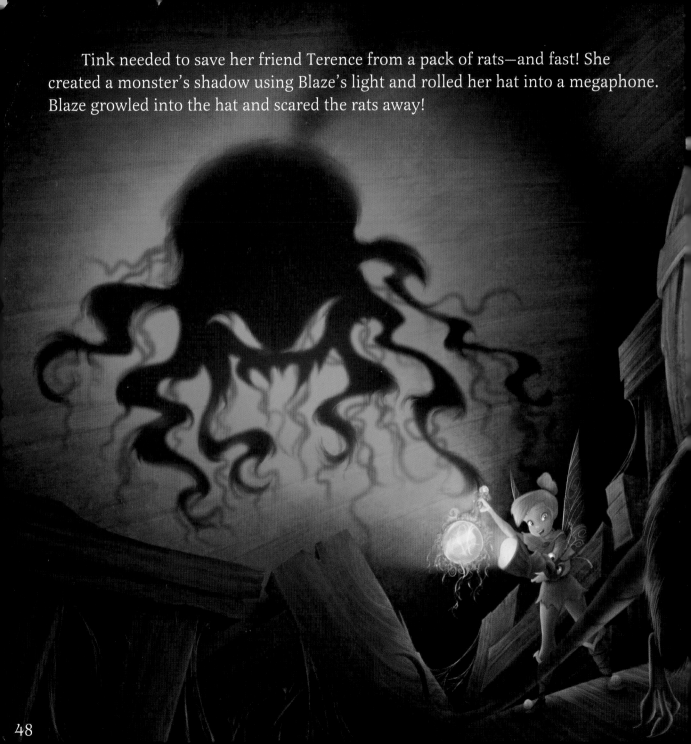

Tink needed to save her friend Terence from a pack of rats—and fast! She created a monster's shadow using Blaze's light and rolled her hat into a megaphone. Blaze growled into the hat and scared the rats away!

Think Fast

You must be quick-thinking
when an adventure gets risky,
or you'll find yourself in trouble.

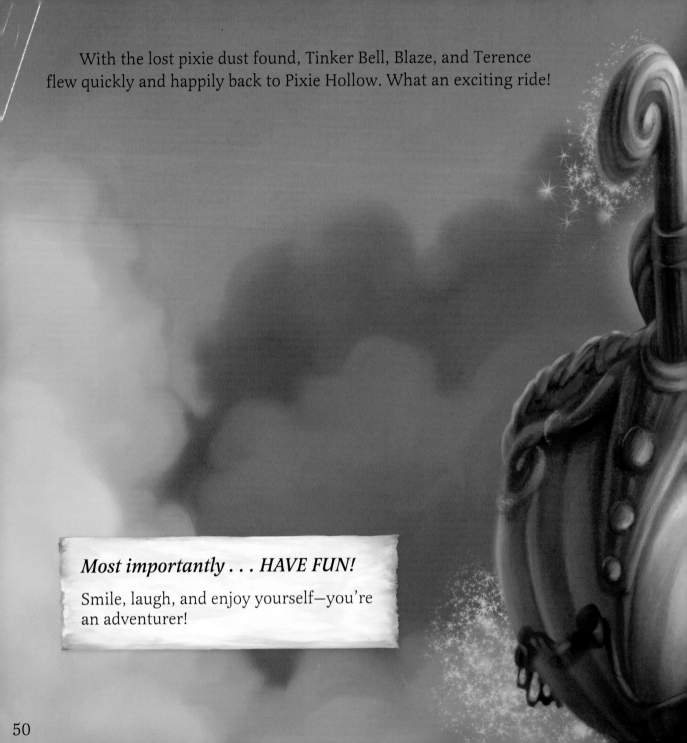

With the lost pixie dust found, Tinker Bell, Blaze, and Terence flew quickly and happily back to Pixie Hollow. What an exciting ride!

Most importantly . . . HAVE FUN!

Smile, laugh, and enjoy yourself—you're an adventurer!

No matter how tiny you are, no adventure is too big—especially when you have good friends by your side. Happy adventuring!

Tinker Bell
AND THE GREAT FAIRY RESCUE

Fairy Rescue Team

Adapted by Kimberly Morris
Illustrated by the Disney Storybook Artists

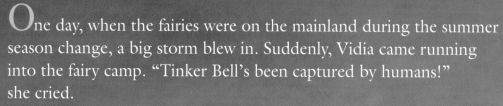

One day, when the fairies were on the mainland during the summer season change, a big storm blew in. Suddenly, Vidia came running into the fairy camp. "Tinker Bell's been captured by humans!" she cried.

"What!" the others gasped.

All of Tink's friends—Silvermist, Fawn, Rosetta, Iridessa, Clank, and Bobble—gathered around Vidia. She told them how she and Tinker Bell had left the camp earlier and gone exploring.

"Tinker Bell went into this little house in the meadow and couldn't get back out," Vidia told the others.

The "little house" Vidia was talking about was a fairy house built by a human girl named Lizzy. The girl had hoped it would attract the attention of a curious fairy like Tinker Bell. And it had!

Vidia had followed Lizzy to the big house where she lived. But Vidia soon realized she couldn't save Tink by herself. She would have to get help.

Tinker Bell's friends started planning a rescue right away. The rain made it impossible for them to fly—water makes fairy wings too heavy. They decided to build a boat out of bark and reeds. If they couldn't fly to the rescue, they would *sail* to the rescue.

It was a dangerous journey. Floodwaters swirled around them.
Fawn climbed to the top of the mast to see what was ahead. Oh,
no! They were headed straight for a waterfall. If they went over,
they would crash into the rocks below!

Silvermist, the water fairy, knew just what to do. "Rosetta, come grab my feet," she said.

With Rosetta holding on to her ankle, Silvermist leaned out of the boat and touched the raging water with her fingertips.

Using all of her water-fairy magic and strength, Silvermist made a water bridge. The passengers held on for dear life as the boat shot down this new pathway of water, avoiding the waterfall. It was a wild ride!

The boat zoomed over the jagged rocks and crashed into a bank of tall weeds. None of the fairies was injured, but the boat was destroyed.

"Looks like we're walking from here," Vidia said.

"But walking where?" Fawn asked.

"There's no way of knowing which way to go," Clank moaned.

The fairies were lost!

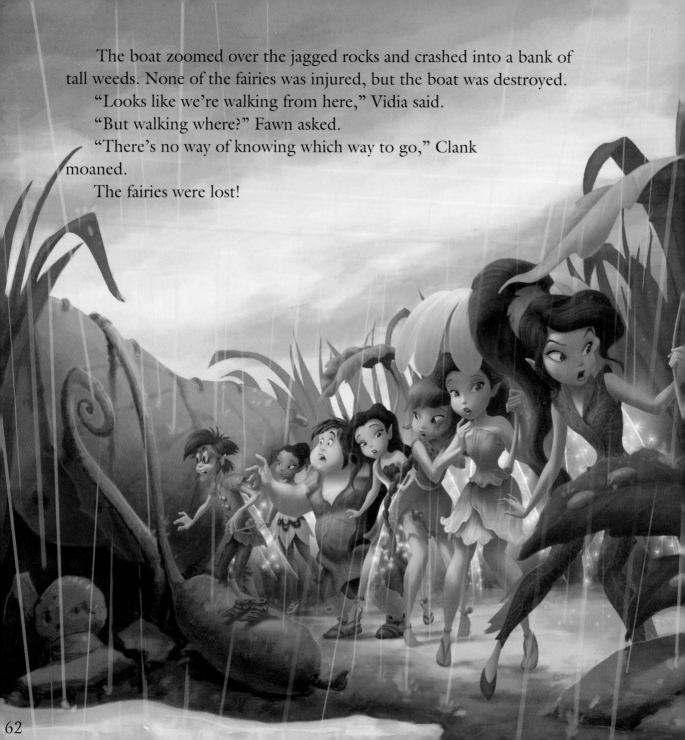

Just then, Vidia looked at the ground and saw
a trail of buttons—the same buttons that had led
Tinker Bell to the fairy house.

"I know where we are!" Vidia announced
happily.

Vidia led the group through the high grass to a road. But the road was flooded. She bravely jumped in and landed in muddy water up to her knees. "It's not deep," she said. "We could walk across."

One by one, the others walked through the icky mud. But when it was Rosetta's turn, she shook her head. "I don't really do mud," she told them.

"But you're a garden fairy," Vidia argued.

Rosetta realized she had no choice. She took off her sandals and stepped daintily across. "Ew! Squishy!" she complained.

With everyone safely across, it was Vidia's turn to get out of the road. But when she tried to move, she sank deeper into the mud. Vidia was stuck!

Then the fairies heard the sound of a car and saw headlights speeding toward them. The car was aimed right for Vidia! The other fairies tried to pull her free, but it was no use.

This time, it was Iridessa, the light fairy, who came to the rescue. Iridessa held out her hands and caught the glare from the headlights in her palms. Using her fairy magic, she bent the light back toward the car.

The driver saw the light and thought a motorcycle was coming toward him. At the last second he veered to the side, barely missing the fairies.

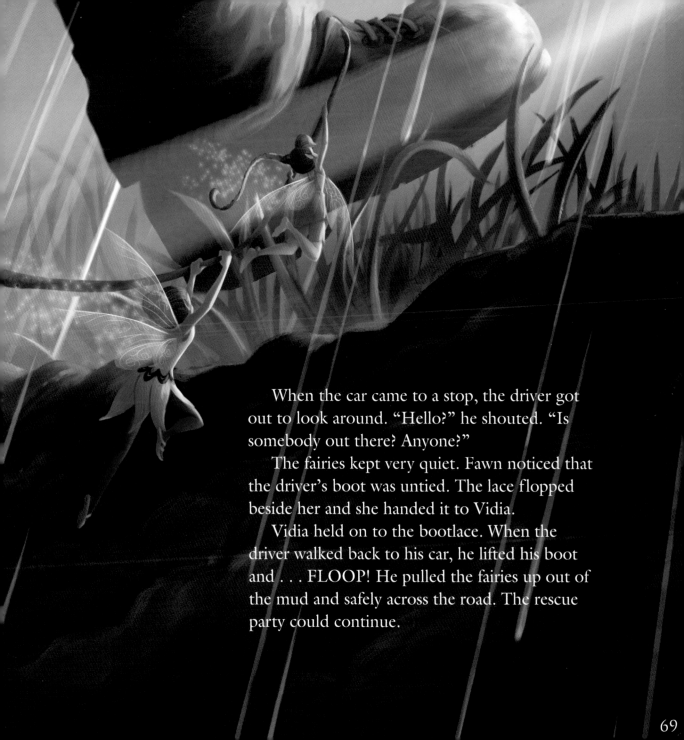

When the car came to a stop, the driver got out to look around. "Hello?" he shouted. "Is somebody out there? Anyone?"

The fairies kept very quiet. Fawn noticed that the driver's boot was untied. The lace flopped beside her and she handed it to Vidia.

Vidia held on to the bootlace. When the driver walked back to his car, he lifted his boot and . . . FLOOP! He pulled the fairies up out of the mud and safely across the road. The rescue party could continue.

As the group got closer to their destination, Vidia grew more worried. She had a guilty secret, and she couldn't keep it to herself any longer. "Listen, there's something you all should know," she told the others. "Tinker Bell getting trapped is my fault."

Vidia admitted that she had slammed the door of the little house and then hadn't been able to get it open. "Now I've put us all in danger. I am so sorry."

The others reminded Vidia that Tinker Bell was *always* getting into trouble. Getting Tink *out* of trouble sometimes felt like a full-time job. They were glad to have Vidia as part of the team.

The girls put their hands together and invited Vidia to join them in their special friendship pledge. "Faith, trust, and pixie dust," they all recited.

The fairies kept going through the dark and rainy night. When they reached the house where Lizzy lived, they sneaked into the kitchen. Vidia told them to be very careful. Not only did they need to watch out for the little girl and her father, they also needed to watch out for a cat.

"Cat?" Iridessa gasped. "What cat?"

"*That* cat!" Clank and Bobble wailed.

Just then, Mr. Twitches, the cat, came in. He was wet. And he was angry. The fairies backed into a corner and Mr. Twitches pounced!

The fairies scattered in every direction. Clank landed on a shelf and sprinkled pixie dust on all the cups and saucers.

The dishes floated into the air and the fairies jumped aboard, spinning around the kitchen. That was when Fawn spotted a plant on the windowsill. "Rosetta, is this what I think it is?"

"Darling, that's exactly what you think it is—catnip!"

Clever Fawn used all her animal-fairy magic—plus a little bit of the catnip—to tame Mr. Twitches. A few whiffs turned him into a real pussycat. Everybody climbed aboard the happy kitty and prepared to find Tinker Bell.

But they didn't have to go far . . .

. . . because at that moment, Tink came into the kitchen with Lizzy.

"Tinker Bell!" the fairies shouted.

The rescue was a success! The fairies knew that after the rain stopped, it was going to be a wonderful summer—not just for them, but also for Lizzy, the little girl who believed in fairies.